Allosaurus
The troublesome tooth

Written by Catherine Veitch
Illustrated by Steve Brown

Miles Kelly

Once, there was a young Allosaurus called Ava who had a huge mouth full of big, pointy teeth.

Ava was very proud of her teeth.
She was always opening her mouth wide
to show them off to her friends.

But one day Ava wasn't feeling well, and didn't flash her toothy smile at anyone.

"What's wrong?" asked her mum.

"I gok oof ake," mumbled Ava.

Poor Ava had **toothache** and didn't feel like playing with her friends.

"I hink I'll sit own under this ush," said Ava.

Next, Ava's friend Cody the Caudipteryx came looking for her.

"Ava!" cried Cody. "Can you come out to play?"

"Ooooooow," shook the bush.

Cody thought the noise must be the wind blowing through the bushes.

"Oooooooow," it went again, but much louder this time.

"Yikes!" screamed Cody. "That bush is alive!" And he ran away as fast as he could.

A bit later, Shay the Suchomimus walked past the bush, looking for Ava.

"Grrrrrrrrr!" the bush rattled.

Shay thought the noise might be a monster. "Grrrrrrrrrr," came the noise again, and the bush started to move.

"Help!" screamed Shay. "That bush is alive and it's coming after me!"

The **bush monster** shuddered and shook as it ran after Shay. Then as flowers and leaves fell off, Ava appeared.

"Ick's me!" Ava spluttered, "I nok a mon ser!"

Nina and Cory rushed to where all the noise was coming from.

Ava told her friends that she had crawled under the bush because of her toothache.

"Try chewing on a gingko leaf," said Nina. "That helps me."

Ava didn't really like to eat leaves. But she **chewed** and **chomped** on the bitter leaf. Every time she chewed with her bad tooth it still hurt.

"Try gargling with water," said Cody.
And he dipped an **empty shell** in a
puddle and filled it with
the cool water.

Shay was hunting for something on the leafy ground.

"Ah, found one!" he said, and he held up a **big bone**. "Try crunching on that!"

Ava crunched and crushed the bone into pieces in her mouth.

CRACK! CRUNCH!

But every time she bit on the side of her poorly tooth, it hurt.

Ava went home. Nothing had stopped her toothache. **She was sad.**

"Maybe Grandpa can help?" said her mummy.

So Ava went to see her Grandpa.

Ava told Grandpa everything she had tried to cure her toothache...

She had **chewed** a gingko leaf...
gargled with cold water...
and even **crunched** on a bone.

"Open wide," said Grandpa.

Grandpa almost put his whole nose in Ava's mouth to get a good look at her bad tooth.

"Go home and try to sleep," said Grandpa. "I think that tooth may fix itself very soon," he said.

The next morning as Ava opened her mouth wide to check her bad tooth, **out it popped!**

"My toothache has gone!" beamed Ava. "And soon I will have a shiny, **new tooth!**"